The Eig
Reindeer Monologues

by

Jeff Goode

Baker's Plays
7611 Sunset Blvd.
Los Angeles, CA 90046
bakersplays.com

NOTICE

This book is offered for sale at the price quoted only on the understanding that, if any additional copies of the whole or any part are necessary for its production, such additional copies will be purchased. The attention of all purchasers is directed to the following: this work is fully protected under the copyright laws of the United States of America, the British Commonwealth, including Canada, and all other countries of the Copyright Union. Violations of the Copyright Law are punishable by fine or imprisonment, or both. The copying or duplication of this work or any part of this work, by hand or by any process, is an infringement of the copyright and will be vigorously prosecuted.

This play may not be produced by amateurs or professionals for public or private performance without first submitting application for performing rights. Royalties are due on all performances whether for charity or gain, or whether admission is charged or not. Since performance of this play without the payment of the royalty fee renders anybody participating liable to severe penalties imposed by the law, anybody acting in this play should be sure, before doing so, that the royalty fee has been paid. Professional rights, reading rights, radio broadcasting, television and all mechanical rights, etc. are strictly reserved. Application for performing rights should be made directly to BAKER'S PLAYS.

No one shall commit or authorize any act or omission by which the copyright of, or the right to copyright, this play may be impaired. No one shall make any changes in this play for the purpose of production.

Publication of this play does not imply availability for performance. Both amateurs and professionals considering a production are strongly advised in their own interest to apply to Baker's Plays for written permission before starting rehearsals, advertising, or booking a theatre.

Whenever the play is produced, the author's name must be carried in all publicity, advertising and programs. Also, the following notice must appear on all printed programs, "Produced by special arrangement with Baker's Plays."

Licensing fees for THE EIGHT: REINDEER MONOLOGUES is based on a per performance rate and payable one week in advance of the production. Please consult the Baker's Plays website at www.bakersplays.com or our current print catalogue for up to date licensing fee information.

Copyright © 1997 by Jeff Goode

Made in U.S.A.
All rights reserved.

THE EIGHT: REINDEER MONOLOGUES
ISBN 978-0-87440-050-2
168-B

PRODUCTION HISTORY

The first public performance of *The Eight: Reindeer Monologues* was in a staged reading December 18, 1993 by the Hidden Theatre, Chicago, IL. The cast was as follows:

DASHER .... Jeff Goode
CUPID .... Foster MacLean
HOLLYWOOD .... Michael Steffens-Moran
BLITZEN .... Jen Moses
COMET .... Doug Steckel
DANCER .... Jennifer Bills
DONNER .... James Finney
VIXEN .... Inger Hatlen

A workshop production of *The Eight: Reindeer Monologues* was staged on August 27, 1994 by Dolphinback Theatre Company, Chicago, IL. The director was Patrick Siler. The cast was as follows:

DASHER .... Phil Gigante
CUPID .... Todd Wm. Ristau
HOLLYWOOD .... Ian Christopher
BLITZEN .... KellyAnn Corcoran
COMET .... Greg Werstler
DANCER .... Beth Stephenson
DONNER .... Michael Dowd
VIXEN .... Melanie Dix

The Eight: Reindeer Monologues premiered November 27, 1994 with the following theatre companies:

Adobe Theatre Company
(New York City, NY)

Directed by Jeremy Dobrish

DASHER .... James McCauley
CUPID .... Frank Ensenberger
HOLLYWOOD .... Vin Knight
BLITZEN .... Kathryn Langwell
COMET .... David Troup
DANCER .... Julie Kessler
DONNER .... Arthur Aulisi
VIXEN .... Erin Quinn Purcell

Stephanie Kim	Costume Designer
Matthew Maraffi	Set Designer
Stephanie McCormick	Production Stage Manager
Chris Todd	Sound Design
Burke Wilmore	Lighting Designer
Christopher Marobella	Antler Design
Erin Quinn Purcell	Assistant Director
Mark Hunter	Assistant Stage Manager
Christopher Roberts	Production Manager
Lance Ball	Asst. Prod. Manager
Amanda Silberstein	Costume Assistant
Stephanie Brunson	Light Board Op
Michelle Mazzarino	Sound Board Op
Eric Cline	Artwork Design
Lisa Maizlish	Photography
Craig Riverside	Program Design

The Source Theatre Company
(Washington, D.C.)

Directed by Joe Banno

CUPID / HOLLYWOOD .... Jim Ferris
BLITZEN / DANCER .... Jeannette Simpson
DASHER / COMET / DONNER .... Gary Telles
VIXEN .... Emily Townley

Costume Designer   Joan A.S. Lada
Assistant Director   Haley Murphy
Stage Manager   John "Scooter" Krattenmaker

Midwest Center for Developing Artists
(Iowa City, IA)

Directed by Todd Wm. Ristau

DASHER .... James Thorn
CUPID.................................... Todd Ristau
HOLLYWOOD .... Seán Judge
BLITZEN .... Cheryl Snodgrass
COMET .... Brant Peitersen
DANCER .... Stephanie Frey
DONNER .... Kris Farrar
VIXEN .... Tina Howard

Light Board Operator   Don Shalley

Dolphinback Theatre Company
(Chicago, IL)

Directed by Patrick Siler

DASHER .... Phil Gigante
CUPID.................................... Joe D. Russell
HOLLYWOOD .... Tom Gottlieb
BLITZEN......................... KellyAnn Corcoran
COMET .... Gregory Werstler
DANCER .... Marie Vlasin
DONNER .... Michael Dowd
VIXEN .... Beth Stephenson

Co-Director	Beth Stephenson
Production Manager	Gregory Werstler
Stage Manager	Jason Fabiani
Props/Scenic Design	Shauna Hudson
Props/Scenic Design	Gretchen Massey
Lighting Coordinator	Michael McNamara
Costumes Coordinator	Michele Friedman Siler
Comet Posters & Publicity Art	Ian Christopher

Hudson Backstage
(Hollywood, CA)

Directed by Allison Gendreau

DASHER .... Frank Gallagher
CUPID................................... Michael Walsh
HOLLYWOOD Benjamin John Parrillo / Brian Ruf
BLITZEN.................................... Erin Fiedler
COMET .... Richard Augustine
DANCER .... Victoria Delaney
DONNER .... Brian Hall
VIXEN .... Allison Gendreau

Assistant Director	Christine Romeo
Music	Alan Axelrod
Lighting	Michael 'Gator' Lawrence

Brave Hearts Theatre
(Madison, WI)

Directed by Cheryl Snodgrass

DASHER .... Brian Bon Durant
CUPID.................................. Daniel Dennis
HOLLYWOOD/PRANCER .... Jay Fricke
BLITZEN ....Johanna Pinzler
COMET .... Matthew Tallman
DANCER .... Emily Joy Weiner
DONNER .... Chris Babiarz
VIXEN .... Clare Riordan

Costumes/Stage Manager	Juliette Willis
Assistant Director	Dara Kennan
Set Designer	Jacob Harlow
Lighting Designer	Joshua Williamson
Technical Director	C.B. Hay
Run Crew	Matt Miller

Dedicated to

Hannah Gale
Inger Hatlen
Meghan Schumacher
Oliver Oertel
Greg Jackson
and
Melissa Flaim

for believing in this play
before
it was written

Thank you.

CHARACTERS

DASHER
CUPID
HOLLYWOOD
BLITZEN
COMET
DANCER
DONNER
VIXEN

THE EIGHT
Reindeer Monologues

DASHER

My name is Dasher.

First reindeer.

From day one.

"Number one from day one."

I been makin' the Christmas run longer than *anyone*
except the fatboy himself.

I've been *the* reindeer,
every year,
for as long as reindeer could fly.

So I don't have to put up with this shit.

One time
I was not the lead reindeer.
One time.

One ...
foggy Christmas Eve.
Yeah, right.
Fine, whatever, I don't want to talk about it.

Just that one time
he was the lead reindeer.

And what did it get him?

And where am I?
RIGHT BACK AT THE FRONT OF THE PACK
the very next year.
And every year since.

So you wanna tell me it was fog?
Fine, it was fog, I'm not challenging that.
And I don't wanna talk about it anyway.

All I'm saying ...

All I'm saying
is 'Fog, my reindeer ass.'

I have seen blizzards
and torrents of freezing rain and sleet
and lightning
on Christmas Eve.

I have seen
an ice
tornado.
Jagged shards of ice
like broken glass whipping through the air
like bullets.
Blood
all over our bodies
from being all cut up.
And it's freezing cold.
And the wind.
And we were pulling two short
because Blitzen
and The Faggot
stayed home.
They didn't wanna go.
'Unsafe working conditions.'
My fuzzy ass! They were chicken shits.

12

They knew it was bad.
They knew something was gonna go wrong.
They had the funny feeling you get in your antlers
when there's gonna be an earthquake,
or when something's just gonna go down ugly.

And it did.

That was the year we lost what's-his-name.
The guy Hollywood replaced,
Vixen's mate.
Victor.

His hind leg was cut up real bad
from this weird ice storm.
And when we came down too heavy
on one of those real steep gabled roofs ...
He slipped.
And his leg just snapped.
Bone sliced right through an artery ...
He was gone before we even knew what happened.

Fatboy just unhitched him.
Left him on that rooftop.
Said, 'Boys, we gotta run to make.'
' ... ho ho ho.'

And we did.

And there was Christmas.

Thanks to the five of us,
and thanks to Victor.
There was Christmas.

He knew it was bad, too.
Victor knew something like this could happen.
But he wasn't sittin' at home saying,
'That's too dangerous.'

"I got a bad feeling."

Every boy and girl on the face of this earth
is counting on us
to bring Christmas joy into their home.
And we got no business
sitting at the North Pole
watchin' TV, saying,
"Glad I'm not out in that."
"I don't get paid for that."
That is exactly what we get paid for!
I can name you fifty flying reindeer right now
who will run on a clear night with temperatures in the
mid 30's.
We
are supposed to be
the Elite.
"The Eight."
There's a problem? We handle it.

Fog?

I will take the risk
of flying head first
into the side of a skyscraper that wasn't there last year.
I've done it before.
Three times.
And am I accusing someone else
of ... unChristmaslike behavior?
No I am not.
My risk, my problem.
And it doesn't matter anyway
because I survived it.
I'm still here.
Still at the front.
Still runnin'.
This year, next year, and every year.

So you wanna hear my story?

I don't know what happened.

I don't know,
and I don't *want* to know.

So when I hear all this whining.

When I see lawyers
runnin''round all over the fuckin' place ...

That's not Christmas.

That's not Christmas,
and that's not taking responsibility
for your own
... whatever, actions.
That's not takin' responsibility, period.

Because we've got a responsibility.
And suppose they do find out something?
What if?
What then?
Do we hand it all over to the elves and walk away?
'Oh, I'm sorry. This shouldn't have happened, I quit.'
'I'm sorry Johnny and Janey and Jamal'
and two billion other kids
all over the world
for whom Santa Claus
is
Christmas.
'I just wasn't happy here!
So you
can never be happy
at Christmas again
for as long as you live ...'

I mean,
what's happened to Rudolph
is very, very ...
very tragic.
But I wanna say this about the kid.
Even after all this,
I know
that if he could,
he would jump
right back in the harness again.
Because that's what you do.

That.
Is what.
You do.

And that is all I'm gonna say to any of you about this.

    (*Blackout.*)

CUPID

Hi, I'm Cupid. *HAHAHA*
The Goddess of Love! *HAHAHA*
I'm sorry, did I say 'Goddess'? God. God of love.
Heeheehee
I never get that straight.

Now what kind of parent
names their kid
after the Roman God of Pornography? *HAHAHA*
It's no wonder I'm screwed up.
I mean, how was I supposed to have a quote-unquote
normal sexual development
when my *name*
is synonymous with Romance.
'Oh, Cupid,
make me quiver
with your magic
shaft of love!'

You know how many times I've heard that in my life?

You know how many times I've said, 'No'?
About half. *HAHAHA*

In fact,
you know who the first person was who ever said that to
me?
... *Mrs. Claus.*
Now *that* was sexual harassment.
I hadn't even hit puberty yet.
I had to go ask someone what she meant.

You know why they call her Mrs. Claus?

(Claw gesture.)

Rrarr.

No, really.
"Oh Santa. Rrarr."
"Dammit woman I was gonna wear that shirt." *HAHAHA*

Just something I overheard.

That is one crazy couple.
Some of the freaky shit they're into even *I* wouldn't
touch.

So this whole thing really comes as no surprise to me.
Some of the Santophiles are skeptical,
but I believe every word of it.

That man has been a walking, talking,
holly-jolly sex crime waiting to happen
for years now.

Do you know
how many tight young asses he's had across his lap?
ALL OF THEM!
EVERY SINGLE ONE.
He makes them stand in line!

(As Santa.)

"Have you been a good little boy or girl? Ho Ho Ho"
"What do you want Santa to give you for Christmas?"
Bouncy Bouncy Bouncy.
"How 'bout a choo choo train?"

(As himself.)

How 'bout a condom?
Or some shark repellant.

Sometimes Santa just gives me the willies.
Well, not me personally.
Santa would never give *me* his willie.
And that
is because he thinks I
might enjoy it. *Hababa*

He would be WRONG in that assumption!

Being gay does *not* mean being
utterly without class, taste or discretion.

Although, somehow, that is the popular
misconception.

But I play into it 'cause it keeps him away from me.
"Ooh Thanta! Red fur again this season?
You know how that makes me *ruff* HaHa!

The last thing I need
is the jolly old elf
coming down my chimney on Christmas Eve.
HAHAHAHAHAHA
That's what he likes to call it:
The jolly old elf.
It's red and white, did you know that?
He had it tattooed.
Little red outfit with white trim. Sound familiar?
When Santa gets a chubby, it looks just like him.
HAHAHAHAHAHA

(*Pointing.*)

Big Santa, little Santa.
And they're *both* lively and quick.
HAHAHAHAHAHAHA

Now, I must repeat,

19

I do not speak from first hand experience.
I think I'm the *only* reindeer Santa *hasn't* tried to
molest.
Why is it that pedophiles are so homophobic?

(Changing the subject.)

And why is it that homophobes think they are God's gift
to gays?
"Oh yes,
you know I want you.
All my life
I've been looking for a greasy fat wifebeater
to abuse me and make me squeal."

He hates me.
I don't know why he doesn't just fire me and get it over
with.
I think it's because he likes to know where I am:
He likes to know that I'm
right there in the third row, between Donner and
Hollywood.
Just far enough away that I don't give him cooties.
But still close enough for the whip.

He loves that whip.

And to tell the truth, I kind of like it, too.
Not as an everyday thing, mind you.
But every once in awhile it's nice.
Adds a little holiday spice to the season.
It's the only thing Santa and I enjoy doing together.
On Dasher, on Dancer! On Cupid and Vixen!
On Comet, on Cupid! On Cupid and Blitzen!

But really, his sadistic zeal is such a waste.
I mean,
don't tell Kris Kringle this,
but I am not the *only* gay reindeer.

What would be the point?
If you're gay and nobody else is,
then you're not really gay. You're a monk.
No, that's a bad example.
Well you know what I mean.
I'm just not the only gay reindeer.
I'm not even the only one on the team.
But I am the only *openly* gay reindeer.
And I love it.
Hollywood said fame would go to my head,
but trust me,
it goes other places. *HAHAHA*

And if anybody asks you why Cupid is gay,
this is what you tell them:
Oral Sex.
Because until you have had a salt lick job
from a full grown reindeer buck,
you have never been to heaven.

Because does are nice —
and I've had my share.
But when a buck gives you snout ...
Oh!
... goring you in the belly with his antlers.
Oh God, it's excruciating.
... *Oh!*

I'm sorry, was I getting a bit bawdy there? I'm sorry.
After all this is a *family* holiday.

... But then, that's what we are.
One big beautiful happy family
with Mommy and Daddy
and all their little children
and everything that goes with it.
Sibling rivalry and favoritism
and little petty quarrels
that grow into the most loathsome hatreds.

21

And Daddy's a workaholic,
and Mommy's an alcoholic,
and little brother's a sodomite,
and little sister's a porno queen.
Chemical dependencies and botched suicide attempts
and repressed memories of sexual abuse and child
molestation
spewing forth at the dinner table over turkey and
cranberry sauce.
And Daddy's a rapist, and Mommy's a vivisectionist,
and they both want a divorce, but they
stay together
for the sake of the children.
But the children don't *want* them together,
the children don't want them at all, they don't want any
of this,
they just want to be far far away
from Mommy and Daddy and all the other children.
But
they stick together anyway,
through thick and thin.
With big gift-wrapped presents at the family holidays
and big blooming bouquets at the family funerals.
And THIS
is what CHRISTMAS
is all about!!

... *HA HA HA HA HA HA HA HA HA HA HA HA HA HA
HA HA HA HA HA HA HA HA HA HA HA HA HA HA HA
HA HA HA HA HA HA HA HA HA HA* Ha Ha Ha Ha Ha Ha
Ha Ha Ha Ha Ha Ha Ha Ha Ha Ha Ha ha ha ha ha ha ha ha
ha ha ha ha ha ha ha ha ha hahahahahahaha hahahahahaha ...

I try not to let it get me down.

   (*Blackout.*)

HOLLYWOOD

They call me
Hollywood.
'The most famous reindeer of all.'
... To borrow a line from Rudolph's
little jingle.
I don't think he'll '*mind*'.

I guess I shouldn't speak ill of the braindead.
I just hate him.
I don't hate *him*.
I hate his movie.
That claymation piece of crap just about ruined my
career.
Did you see it? God, I hope not.
I look terrible.
Flanks out to here.
All of us look terrible, though, because we all look alike.
Santa and his eight tiny clonedeer.

You know why that is?
Every last reindeer in that film looks the same.
Not just The Eight.
Every reindeer in every scene.
Except Rudolph, of course.
All the rest of us look exactly like
Donner.

The *women* look like Donner!
I said this at the time, I said,
'The *does* have antlers.
You can't have does with antlers.'
They said,
'That's okay,
most people don't know there are girls on the team

anyway."
Yeah, sure, people don't know there are girls.
You find me a baby name book that lists Vixen
under "cute nicknames for boys".
Putting antlers on that slut
is like having a centerfold with a pop-up phallus.
SPROING!
That's how I feel every time I see that movie.
SPROING! What the hell am I looking at???
Abominable snowmonster?
Island of misfit toys?
Rudolph speaking without an interpreter?
Continuity in the film industry just makes me cringe.
Like in *my* movie ...

Prancer was supposed to be based on a true story.
But by the time they finished editing it,
it looked like the little girl had saved *my* life.
Can you believe that?
I guess that's what I get for not sitting through rushes.
I'm pretty happy with it though.
At least I wasn't made out of Play-Doh and brown felt.
I said, "No way.
I want live action,
big budget,
and an original score by John Williams."
"*And* I want to play the role myself or I'm not signing
anything."

We almost got John Williams.
He wanted to do it, but he had other commitments.

So I was telling you why Donner got the Rudolph deal ...
Not because he has the best profile.

In order to gloss over his role in the "foggy Christmas"
affair,
Donner wants to make a movie of *his* version
of what was,
quite frankly,
one of the most sordid events in North Pole history.
So he makes phone calls,
writes letters.
And he gets his lips on the ass of every movie exec north
of Anchorage for almost a year
until he finally lands the deal with this Claymation
company.
This outfit is *so* second-rate
that they go over budget flying in a deer from New York
to play Rudolph.
So ...
They aren't going to pay the rest of us!
Well, I walked out.
I said, "Santa, Donner,
if you want me to sell my soul,
you're gonna have to come up with the cash.
Because I only do charity work
once a year."

And everyone else went with me.
And that's why every deer in that movie bears a strange
resemblance to Rudolph's daddy. Terrible movie.
They didn't even ask me to sign a release to use my name!

So this year my agent's getting an injunction to keep
them from airing it.
I'm not trying to be vindictive or anything.
It's just that it hurts the distribution of my movie.
Really.
Video rentals of *Prancer*
go *down* during the holiday season
because that's when the networks air *Rudolph.*
I think that's one reason why I didn't get an Oscar
nomination.

The Rudolph movie and, uh ...
racism in the film industry.
No deer
has ever
been nominated for an academy award.
Are you gonna tell me Bambi
didn't deserve an Oscar?
My god, when his mother died,
I just wept.
Of course, that was animation.
But my movie ...
Live action.
Feature length.
All-star cast: Sam Elliot, Chloris Leachman, Abe Vigoda.
Two years in the making.
... I did my own stunts!
What did I get?

Hello! Motion Picture Academy!
Were you *asleep* during the broken leg scene?
Deserted snow-covered highway,
cold winter night,
broken leg,
Sam Elliot coming at me with a loaded shotgun ...

    (Steps, limps, steps, limps.)

    (Deer moan.)

"WAAUGH!"

Oh!
Give that deer an Oscar.

I'm looking at treatments, now, for the sequel,
but it's tough because there's so much crap out there.
Look at this:

    (Looks at a script.)

'*Prancer II*
Opening sequence.
Night time. Christmas Eve. Winter.'
Now there's an innovation.
'I've got this Christmas Eve story and,
hey, I've got a great idea:
Let's set it in winter!'

'Prancer gets separated from Santa and becomes lost in a
forest.' What *is* this?
'Lost in a forest'?
Why don't I just fly up over the trees and see where I am?
'He arrives in the yard of an orphanage ...' Oh no.
I am *not* working with kids again.
It's absolutely true what they say about
working with children and animals.
They'll steal the scene every time.
Now,
I do it
because I have an uncanny natural sense of the
cinematic,
but children do it
because they're obnoxious and self-centered. I hate
children.
But all of these ideas are like this.
Kids and deer, deer and kids.
Kids and deer and Christmas.

What about a Schwarzenegger/Prancer buddy film?
Arnold plays Santa,
I play myself.
We set it in the year 2000.
Cuban Mafia cyborgs have taken over the North Pole
using virtual reality elf doppelgangers.
Arnold and I go down to Miami to kick some tail.
We wipe out entire Latino crime families
in high tech combat sequences.
We uncover a plot to export stolen nuclear weapons
and soon we're running from crooked cops and robot

27

assassins hired by a European drug cartel bent on world
domination.
Lots of location shooting,
lots of stunts, special effects.
You slot it for a summer release in the United States
and we're talking blockbuster.
There's not a man, woman or child
who won't pay $7.50 to see that.

... I'll probably have to write it myself.

... But, now.
... with this Vixen thing.
... I don't know what's gonna happen.

If she sells her story to a cable network,
it's going to undercut anything I do next year.
You know that's why she's doing it.
They all want to be Hollywood.
Vixen, Donner, all of them.
That's why this is coming out right now.
When the media is focussed on us.

We *all*
have Santa Claus stories.
Most of us have a few Vixen stories, too.
She was *also*
'no saint'.

We all have stories.
Most of us
just have the common courtesy not to share them
with the wrong people at the wrong time
when someone else's
career is on the line.

The *only* thing we don't all have ...

    (He points at himself.)

28

... is talent.
And that's where she's made her big mistake.
Because six months from now
when HBO starts filming
The Vixen Story: Holly and Harassment.
See if they ask *her* to play herself in the movie.
This little uproar is going to get her nowhere.
Which is why I am not cooperating with this
investigation. There are things I know.
There are things I don't know.
But I have nothing to gain
by Vixen's little tell-all scheme.
And until I do ...
She can cry all she wants.

Oh! And, I almost forgot,
this Friday 8 o'clock NBC,
Hollywood Goes To Hollywood: The Making of Prancer.

Wonderful behind-the-scenes footage. Don't miss it.

   (*Blackout.*)

BLITZEN

The sleigh ride is over.

It looks like Santa Claus has finally gone too far.
Sure,
he's acting surprised and confused
and hurt by the allegations.
That doesn't mean he's innocent.
It means he's crossed that line so many times
that he's forgotten it's wrong.
He didn't know he *could* go too far.
After all,
hasn't the jolly old elf brought joy
to generations of boys and girls
the world over?

Well,
I hate to break this news to you.
But it isn't *joy*
that makes those children stop believing in Santa Claus
when they hit adolescence.

It's fear.

How many times have we heard it?

"There is no Santa Claus.
Mommy and Daddy bring us the presents
and stuff our stockings,
and drink up the rum and cookies that we leave for
Santa."

It's not because they're growing up.
It's because they're in the first stages
of severe repression.

Ask them where do all the presents come from?
'Daddy hides them in the attic.'
How does he know what to bring you?
'Mommy opens my letters to Santa Claus.'
... How come the *radio stations*
say they've spotted eight tiny radar blips
coming from the North Pole???
'A hoax, an incredible hoax.'

Any psychiatrist will tell you,
this kind of irrational denial
only comes in the face of a reality
too horrible to even think about.
The reality
that a jolly fat pervert is comin' to town.

It's better to believe that your own mother
is committing a Federal crime ...
Than to believe in a grotesque
libidinous troll of a man,
who knows when you are sleeping,
knows when you're awake,
knows how to get into your house, into your room.
And knows that no matter what he does to you,
you won't tell.
Because no one in the world will believe you.
If it's your word against his.

'Molested?
By the man who brought you that nice dolly you always
wanted?
I don't think so.
You'd better watch out,
or he'll think you're a bad little girl
and next year you'll get coal in your stocking.'

So they don't say anything.
And they try to convince themselves that it didn't
happen.

It didn't happen.

But that doll
ends up broken
by dinner time on Christmas day.
And children cry,
on the happiest day of the year.

It's all becoming clear, now, isn't it?

And the rape
of Vixen
is going to be the turning point
in his legacy of perversion,
because you can talk about
good deeds and tradition and holiday spirit
and Santa's work with children and his merry disposition
and "he seems like such a nice fellow"
till your face turns blue,
and *none of that* ...
answers this one question:

Why
would Vixen
lie?

What does she have to gain?

She is one of the eight
highest-ranking reindeer
in the world.
She has sacrificed her family,
her husband Victor to this job.
And now,
all of a sudden
she's going to put her career on the line?
Not even on the line. She's thrown it away.
The conservative press will make sure she never works
again.

After all these years,
she's thrown her career away.

For what?

A prank?
P.M.S.?
No.

She's standing up to him
because what Santa Claus did to her
is wrong.
And the world needs to know it.

A reindeer has a right to her own body!
Why are we treated like livestock??

Why
do we make the Christmas run
wearing nothing but leather straps and jingle bells??
It's not how *I* dress in everyday life.
Why,
when I'm being harnessed to the sleigh,
are the toymaker elves trying to feel me up??
They don't have hormones,
they don't have penises.
They do it because they've seen Santa do it,
they think it's cool.

And it's not just him.

Why can't I walk through a herd of bucks
during mating season
without feeling like piece of venison??

Why do *some* people send me fan mail
that is so obscene
it should just say
'Dear Blitzen's vagina' at the top??

'Cuz they're not talkin' to me.

Why?
WHY?

Santa Claus
has to be punished,
because that will tell the world
that when a Doe says 'No',
it means 'No'.
And when she says, 'Wait',
it means 'No'.
And when she says nothing at all.
... It means 'No'.

And when she says 'Yes'?

Well, this year she's saying 'No'.
'No' to Santa Claus.
'No' to Christmas.
'No' to pretending like nothing happened.

This Christmas Eve,
if Santa Claus is sitting in that sleigh-full-of-toys,
then it is not going up.
I will not fly,
Cupid will not fly,
Vixen will not fly,
Dasher can pull the damn thing by himself if he wants to.

But the rest of us
will not be in front of it.

And it's going to be a sorry Christmas morning
for anyone who thinks this kind of thing can just be
overlooked.

Yes.
I am angry!

If I had been the one he cornered in that toyshop ...
... I would have hoofed him right in the jolly old elf.
He'd be 'HoHoHo-ing' a few octaves up, if it were me.
And I still think that's a viable option.
Neuter Claus
would be a lot easier to work with on those cold winter
nights.
So, yes,
there will be criminal charges.
And don't talk to me about
the 'Institution of Santa Claus'.
An institution doesn't feel.
An institution doesn't suffer.
An institution
doesn't have to look in the mirror
and see how pain has changed it's victim's face.
The victim does.

And no matter how much good Santa Claus has done in
the world.
And it's not as much as you think.
There are still third world countries we don't visit.
And why is that?
Because it cuts costs and nobody cares.
If Santa doesn't visit
Cambodia,
Pakistan,
black South Africa,
who's gonna complain?
Oh, but send in the U.N. troops and he'll be there in a
heartbeat.

(Smiling and waving.)

'Ho Ho Ho, CNN!'

No matter how much good Santa Claus has done,
it does not justify ruining anyone's life.

And if you still think I'm overreacting.
'Because I'm a woman.'
Then go ask Vixen yourself.

No, actually, don't.

Go ask Rudolph.
He won't talk.
He won't *tell* you what caused his relapse.
But you can look at him
standing there in his padded cell.
Mumbling to his invisible friends.
Babbling about mistletoe and penises.
And crying.
And then tell me he shouldn't be stopped.

If we can't make this holiday safe for the children ...
Then, no.
I don't care if we never have Christmas again.

   (*Blackout.*)

COMET

Saint Nicholas saved my life.
He saved my life.

When I was a young buck
I fell in with a bad crowd.
'Hell's Herd'.
Meanest fawns in the Northern Hemisphere,
bar none.
We'd go out drinking every night.
Getting in fights.
Knocking over igloos.
One time an Eskimo called us herbivores.
We sank his kayak.
Back then, I used to have this tattoo on my shoulder
of a flaming deer skull
with a fiery tail
like a comet.
That's how I got my nickname:

Skull.

I don't have it anymore,
I had it branded over.
Now it's a snowcone.
Saint Nick helped me put those days behind me.

When you hear stories of young deer gone bad.
That was me.
We would roam the range.
Lookin' for trouble.
There isn't much trouble on the range though,
so one winter night ..
We went into the city.
We were high on cocaine.

Flying between buildings.
Zooming in low over the traffic.
City people think they're tough,
but they lose their shit
when they see flying reindeer coming at their
windshield.

Let me tell you,
you don't know the meaning of the word 'tough'
until you've carved your name into a brick wall
using nothing but the bones on your head
and a shot of gin for anaesthetic.

And then we tried to rob a liquor store.

By this time, I was so blind wasted,
I didn't know what I was doing.
It could have been the coke and the fifth of gin I'd had,
but I think it was that bad marijuana.
You see, none of us had smoked pot before and we
wanted to try it. Smoking it, I mean.
We were no strangers to the evil weed.
But out in the wild you just eat it off the bush.
So this roll-it-up-in-paper-and-burn-it thing was a
novelty,
it sounded like fun.

So we beat up a couple of junkies.

And they must have had some bad shit
because when I walked into that liquor store,
all of a sudden these fireworks went off.
And while I'm standing there staring at the pretty colors,
the shopkeeper blasted me
with the .22 he kept under the counter.

They turned me in to the animal shelter,
I couldn't do nothin', I was still delirious.
They thought I was rabid,

they were going to put me down.

But somebody had heard about Saint Nick's work with
troubled deer
and they called him in.
He took me out of there
and he really turned my life around.
He gave me a job,
helped me straighten out.
And now every time I read about one of these young
bucks today.
Gored to death in gang fights.
Or getting drunk and stepping in front of a pick up.
I think,
that could have been me.
That was me.
And the only thing that's kept me from being
just another roadkill ...
Just another nameless face on somebody's trophy room
wall ...
is Saint Nicholas.
And there's no one here who can't say the same.
Ask them.
Ask Dasher.
Ask Dancer.
Ask Prancer where his "career" would be
without The Eight at the top of his resume.
Ask Cupid what *he* was doing before the Kringles took
him in.
Ask him if he'd like to go back.

They'll tell you none of that matters. But it does.
It all matters.
Because Saint Nick has built his life on helping others.
And that makes this kind of accusation such a travesty.

You listen to Blitzen's feminist ranting
and she wants you to forget
that this is the man
who established the first reindeer team in the world
to admit does and bucks on an equal basis.
You want to talk about sexual harassment,
talk to the elves.
They were towel boys
in an Irish brothel when Saint Nick found them.
But he took them out of there,
and set up the toymaker apprenticeship program
so they could retrain,
learn skills they could use.
He sponsors Big Brothers/Big Sisters of America,
the Special Olympics,
UNICEF. All this,
and the Christmas run.
And when you hear what they're saying about Vixen.
Or the latest version of the Rudolph story,
it just doesn't sound like the same man.
Because it's not,
it's not the same man, it's two different men.
One of them is a lie.
And the other is the real Saint Nick.

Rudolph
was just a poor,
deformed,
retarded little reindeer buck
and Saint Nick gave him a chance to be somebody.
To be important.
He showed him that someone had faith in him
when no one else did,
not even his own father.
No, he didn't really lead the team.
But I don't see how you can interpret that
as some sort of conspiracy that ...
that years later has caused him to suddenly
lapse into a catatonic stupor.

40

When the gossip-mongers take Saint Nick's generosity
toward Rudolph
and try to turn it into something warped and perverted,
it just makes me angry.
How can they do that?
It just doesn't make any sense.

Or maybe it makes perfect sense, doesn't it?
Maybe we should be asking *Vixen* what happened to
Rudolph.
I mean, after all,
who is it that's really pushing these perverted
accusations?
The perverts.
Vixen, Blitzen and Cupid.
The two Lesbians and the fag.

Some people don't want to think they're Lesbians, but
they are.
Have you seen the way they look at each other?
Like they know something the rest of us don't?
Well, you don't have to believe me,
but just because they both used to have mates
does not mean they've never gone doe-to-doe.
At the very least, they're all three bisexual,
and they won't be happy until the whole world is
bisexual,
even if that means smearing the reputation
of the one man
who stands for right and good in the
world
and peace on earth and family values.

And that is what I mean when I call them perverts,
because I'm not one to judge anyone's lifestyle,
but ruining a person's good name
to serve your own political agenda,
especially a man who has done so much for so many,
and for you personally,

that is warped.
It's more than warped,
it's un ... *fathomable*.
And it's not in the Christmas spirit.

Really I shouldn't even let it upset me,
it's so ridiculous
I wish I could just sit back and laugh it off.
"Ho ho ho. Saint Nicholas did what? You're joking!"

But that's why I'm not laughing,
because it's not a joke,
they're serious, they're dead serious.
They think they're going to get somewhere with these
charges.
They think they're gonna do the world a favor
and get rid of Saint Nicholas.
Well, it won't be the first time someone has tried.
The world is full of crazies.
It seems like every Christmas there's something new.
Some mother claiming he's molested her child,
because she doesn't want to admit it might be her
husband,
or her new boyfriend.
Or razor blades in their stockings.
Or someone pissing down their chimney.
But nothing has ever been proved.

I guess being a living saint
makes you a target for this kind thing.
But what scares me about *this time*,
this thing with Vixen that everyone is talking about ...
is that some people believe them.
No, no, what *scares* me
is that some people *listen* to them,
that they lend them *any* kind of credibility.
That they don't just walk out of the room
when someone starts talking about it.

Back in the '50s
if someone had said she was raped by Saint Nicholas.
No one would have believed her.
No one would have listened to her.
She would be the one brought up on charges.
But now ...

The fact that people are even listening scares the hell out
of me.
The fact that people want to know the truth,
the fact that I am being asked this question at all,
scares the hell out of me.
Did Saint Nicholas sexually assault one of the reindeer?
How can you ask me that?
How can you even think it?
You know the answer.
He is a good man.
They didn't make him a Saint for his looks.
I'm not trying to be disrespectful, but that's the way it is.

Joan of Arc, Saint Patrick ... glamour Saints.
But the Catholic Church
did not elect Nicholas to Sainthood because he was
glamorous.
They did it because behind that bowlful of jelly
is a heart of gold.
Well, behind it and up a little.
And if he's not perfect,
if he's overweight and out of shape.
if he drinks a little,
It's because he's under a lot of pressure all the time,
and not just on Christmas Eve.
It's because he doesn't spend his money
on health club memberships and personal trainers.
It's because he's not in the company gym every day
playing racquetball between meetings like some of these
lawyers.
And if he doesn't always put the reindeer demands for
better work conditions at the top of his priority list,

it's because there *are* higher priorities.
Saint Nick wasn't put on this Earth to make the eight of
us happy. He wants to make the whole world happy.
And if he can only do that one day out of the year ...
Well it's because of people like this.
Like Vixen,
like Blitzen.
It's because of these journalists
who care more about news-that-sells than news-that's-
true.
It's because of these lawyers
who will courageously fly in the face of tradition
if there's money in it for them.
And it's because of people everywhere all over the world
sitting and watching their televisions in morbid
fascination.
Who don't have the moral fortitude it takes ...
to pick up their remote control
and change the channel.

(Comet mimes a remote control.)

Who don't have the strength of character to say,
'No, I will not listen.'
'No, I will not be a party to this.'
'No, this is not happening.'

No.

(Blackout.)

44

DANCER

This is my favorite Santa Claus story.

When I first came up here after I was offered this
position.
I had no idea this was a Christmas-related job.
And I was looking over my contract, which, of course,
said that we made this run on December 24th, right?
And I'm looking over my contract, and I said,
"What about vacation days?"
And he said,
"You only work one day a year,
you don't get vacation days."
And I said,
"What about sick days and maternity leave?"
And he said
"You don't get sick days, either."
and I said
"What happens if I'm sick on the 24th? Or I'm pregnant?"
And he kind of turned a little red and said,
"You will work the 24th in sickness and in health,
and if you want this job
you will not give birth
on or about the 24th of December."
And I thought, that's a bit fascist.
But I saw he was getting a little hot around the collar, so
I said,
"Okay, fine."
— But secretly I was thinking, we'll just wait and see.
I mean,
if I come in here barfing my lungs out on the 24th
this guy's not going to make me strap on a harness
and fly around the world.
He's got his clients waiting all year for him to make one
delivery,

who's gonna notice if it's postponed a day or two. —

So I'm thinking it over:
no sick days, no vacation days,
but it's only once a year,
and I'm looking at my calendar, and suddenly,
— in a moment of brilliance —
I realize that this is during the holidays.
So then I said,
"So, Mr. Claus
is this scheduled for
sometime around the 24th
most of the time?" And he said,
"No,
it's scheduled for exactly on the 24th
all the time."
And I said,
"Well, not *every* year."
And he said,
"Yes, every fucking year."
Well, I was getting a little pissed off now,
and I said, "Well *excuse me*, Mr. Claus,
but what happens when it falls during
Hanukkah?"
— And I thought that was a reasonable question
because most businesses will give you time off
to spend Hanukkah with your family. —
But he just started laughing that annoying laugh.
And then he said,
"Dancer,
one of my reindeer is a practicing Muslim.
And most of them are devout agnostics.
But on December 24th
you are all Unitarians.
Because on Christmas Eve
I need Christmas deer
to deliver Christmas toys
for Christmas Day."

Boy was I embarrassed.

Comet was a Muslim at the time.
He had just converted to Islam that year.
But then the next summer he made his pilgrimage to
Mecca.
And instead of having this great religious experience
he was completely self-conscious the whole time
because he was the only reindeer there.
And then when people started asking him
what he did for a living
he was afraid to admit that he flew Christmas toys
to good little infidel girls and boys
so he eventually got embarrassed and had to go home ...

So I guess I really have no complaints.

Santa's always been pretty fair with me.

But I've been with The Eight
for a long time.
I know I haven't been here as long as some of them,
like Dasher or
... Vixen.
But I was here before Hollywood came on,
and I was here *way* before Donner and Rudolph.
But I guess we don't count Rudolph.

But if Vixen leaves
and if Blitzen and Cupid go on strike,
then I'll be one of the senior deer
and I was wondering if that means I'll get a pay raise.
I think I should after this.
I mean when someone is raped on the job,
that's a hazardous work environment, right?
You wouldn't see that happening if we worked in a bank.

At least not during business hours.
Or maybe you would, I don't know,

47

I've never worked in a bank.
I was in a zoo for a while,
but the hours are long and the pay is peanuts.
No, that's just a joke. I've never been in a zoo.
I went to one once, and I don't know how those animals
can do it. It's so degrading.
They walk around stark naked
and people take pictures.
And some of them —
and I don't want to sound anti-simian,
but it's mostly the primates —
will stand there
and play with themselves in broad daylight.
And they don't even get tips!
Apparently, zookeepers
don't like people throwing money in the cages.
I guess if you get paid it's pornography,
but if you just get exploited it's family entertainment.

They say Cupid was a zoo-baby.
I think that's why he's like he is,
that's got to be a scarring experience for a young fawn.
Or any child, for that matter.
I just don't understand people.
They'll complain about gratuitous violence
or sex on television or in the movies
and then they'll turn around and take their kids to a
rodeo.
Or a *petting* zoo.
I don't get it.

   (Confidentially.)

If Blitzen —
I'm sorry, I don't mean to change the subject —
If Blitzen and Cupid go on strike
I can't participate.

... I need this job.

48

I used to be a ballet instructor,
and I can't go back to that.
You see, there was a movement —
this was before your time —
a fundamentalist religious movement
where they were saying that reindeer shouldn't ballet.
It was really weird.
There were all these people giving sermons
and talking about it like
a dancing deer was a sign of the apocalypse or something.
I mean,
it's not like we were doing modern dance,
this was classical ballet.
It was really scary.
The only thing I can compare it to
is the holocaust in Germany,
it was scary like that.
Because this whole movement just came at us from out of
nowhere,
deer were beaten to death for wearing tights or a tutu
and we had no idea why it was happening
and we didn't know who to trust
because some of the leaders of the movement were
reindeer.

... They burned my studio.
And I just had to get out.
It was just safer not to dance.
And now nobody does.
And that's why
you've never seen a reindeer ballet.

And it's really tragic, really,
because some of the best dancers in the world at the time
were reindeer.
Ballet just comes naturally to a deer.
Dancing on point.
Breathtaking leaps.

When you see deer *pas de deux*
they can leap over each other's heads.
And of course some of the intricate tailwork
is just gone from the repertoire.
Barishnikov still teaches tailwork,
but it's just not the same.

They used to say that you *had not lived*
until you'd seen a beautiful reindoe
dance *The Nutcracker Suite*
with a flying stag in tights.

I guess nobody lives anymore.

    (Confidentially.)

If I don't —
I'm sorry to change the subject again —
If I don't join the strike,
it's not because I don't believe Vixen.
That day.
Well, I guess Blitzen saw her right afterwards.
And Vixen wouldn't say anything.
But if you'd seen her.
You'd know.
Something happened.

Or maybe not, I don't know,
Santa doesn't really seem like the type to ...
That whole thing with Rudolph is just a story.
Santa never ...
Donner and Santa are very close. I mean ...

I don't know what I mean.

    (Confidentially.)

I don't know why I keep coming back to this, but ...
I was out by the toyshop that day

and I guess I thought ...

I heard strange sounds.
Like screams.

But I didn't think anything of it,
because I've heard strange sounds out by the toyshop
before.

And I just figured it was Santa fighting with Mrs. Claus
again.
They fight all the time.
That woman is just nasty to him.
Especially if she's been drinking.
That's why I don't go to the office Christmas party
anymore.
I tell them it's because I try to keep kosher,
but really it's because Mrs. Claus is always there,
and it's awkward anyway,
because she's the only one who isn't actually involved in
the Christmas run.
She doesn't make toys, she doesn't wrap presents.
She's just Santa's wife, so she comes to the party.
And once she's had too much to drink —
which doesn't take long
because she usually gets started before we even get back
— she starts tossing elves across the room,
or trying to drown them in the punch bowl.
She hates the elves.
I don't know why.
She hates Rudolph, too.
And she never liked me, either.
Is there anyone she doesn't hate?
She likes Cupid.
I'll never understand that, because he insults her to her
face.
One time he said the only thing the Clauses had in
common
were alcoholism,

venereal disease,
and snowy-white beards.
I think she likes some of the bucks.
Comet.
Dasher.

(Confidentially.)

When I —
I'm sorry —
when I first joined the team,
we were getting ready for a trial run
and my sleigh bells weren't fitting properly,
so I went to the toyshop to get another set.
And Santa came in after me,
and he said he wanted to help me try them on.
And I told him I didn't need any help,
but he ...

I don't know ...

And then Dasher came in
and started saying
how beautiful the toys were that year.
... And Santa told him to go away, but he just stood there
looking at Santa and saying,
'What beautiful toys we have.
They seem so very fragile.'
over 'n' over.
Until Santa left ...

(She stares off into her memory ...)

I wish I could dance again.

(Blackout.)

DONNER

I only wanted Rudolph
to have more than I did.

Ya gotta understand:

I was a nothing,
a no deer.

I was never going to pull Santa's sleigh.
I have a bad back.
And I'm not a strong flyer.
And I smoke.

I was an unemployed herd deer.
In fact, I'd been fired from my last job,
and once word gets around that you can't handle
herdwork,
you're through.

So when the vets came to me
and told me my son was going to be born like he was.
That Rudolph would probably never walk without
crutches.
That he would be horribly disfigured
with a face no doe would ever love.
And that he would have the mind of a child
all his life.
And when they told me
that my mate and I shouldn't try to have another,
because our children would all be like that.
Corrie was terribly upset.
But that was the end for me.
That was the end of my life.

Y'see, every parent has dreams for their child.
Dreams that won't ever happen.
That their son
will grow up to be President of the United States.
That their daughter
will maybe grow up to be the President's wife.
Crazy outlandish dreams.
And sometimes,
when your life is where mine was,
the only thing that makes you go on
is that dream
and the hope that your kids
will be better off than you are.
That crazy parental optimism
is what keeps you going through the bad times
when it's a struggle
just to put feed on the table.
Because you know
that even if you never amount to anything,
at least your offspring
have a world of possibilities before them.
And it's worth living another day,
just to see what they do with it.

But Rudolph didn't have any possibilities.
From the moment of his birth,
there was no open country stretched before him
alive with promise.
Only closed doors.

Ya gotta understand,
our whole culture
is based on natural athleticism.
A deer who can't run,
or jump,
or dance, or pull a sleigh.
Or just stand there and look sexy in leather and sleigh
bells.
Is better off dead.

54

If Rudolph were a domestic deer, they would have shot
him,
put him out of his misery.
The only future he ever had
was as a burden to his parents,
who were overburdened enough as it was.

So when Santa gave Rudolph the chance to lead the team.

You bet I jumped at it.
Ya gotta understand what this is like.
The British have their Queen,
Americans have the Beatles.
And reindeer
have The Eight.
I remember once, back before I joined the team,
Victor was making an appearance at a benefit.
I asked him for his autograph
and he misspelled my name.
But for years that autograph was my most prized
possession.
And then when he died, I sold it
and it was enough to pay two months' back rent.
Whoever has that now has one helluva collector's item.

And not just to fly with The Eight,
but to *lead* the team.
Something that only *Dasher* had ever done.
Dasher,
who is like a superhero to most deer.
Dasher,
who flew headfirst
into the World Trade Center,
fell out of his harness,
plummeted sixty stories,

and then jumped right back up
and led the team on to the fastest Christmas run on
record. Dasher,

and Rudolph.

I'm not trying to make excuses.
When Rudolph started telling me that Santa was hanging
around.
Walking him home from school.
Giving him presents.
... I knew what was going on.
And when Rudolph *stopped* telling me about Santa
and just cried.
... I knew what had happened.
And I knew I could have prevented it.

But you never really want to believe something like that
will happen to your own family.
Until it does.

I didn't let Rudolph go out anymore.
We knew Santa waited outside the door.
He stayed home
and his mother and I prayed that it was over.

But when Santa Claus came *into* my house ...

When the most powerful man in the world
came into my home
and asked for my son.
What was I supposed to do?

I did the one thing no one had ever done before.
Many have done it since then,
and most of them will brag about it for the rest of their
lives. But before that day,
no one —
no deer, no elf, nobody —
had ever said, 'No'
to Santa Claus.

I said 'No' to Santa Claus.

He was shocked.
My doe fainted ...
And then ...
He offered me money.
Gifts,
reindeer things.
I said, 'No.'

He told me there was an opening for me on the team.
That my family would never again want for food, or
shelter,
clothing.
That *I,*
Donner,
an unemployed herd deer from Fairbanks,
would be one of the eight most important reindeer in the
world, one of the Dashers,
the Victors,
the Comets.

I said, 'No.'

Then he told me
that he would find a place for Rudolph on the team.
That Rudolph,
who wasn't going to be *anything.*
Who could not have even aspired to be the miserable
failure that his father was.
That Rudolph
who would have been better off dead than born.
Was going to do something
most deer cannot even
dream of.
That, for the first time in his life,
he would have prestige,
power.
That cruelly maimed as he was,
he would never again want for love
or affection.

57

People would write songs about him.
Being the red-nosed reindeer
would be something to be proud of.

"Yes!" I said.
"Yes!"

And I listened to his screams from the next room.
And I listened to his tears for years to come.
But he never again
cried from hunger.
From loneliness.
From humiliation.

Only from fear.
And pain.
And eventually,
after Santa lost interest in him,
he didn't even cry from that.

Those were good years ...

And everyone wants to know how Donner
can work for Santa Claus
after what he's done to my family
and to so many others.

Well, the others are on their own,
but I have made him pay.
I made him pay me.
I made him pay Rudolph.
I make him pay
every time someone else tells him, "no".

And you gotta understand,
I've paid, too.
I paid with my son.
With my mate, who left me.
With my honor and self-respect.

And now,
when I thought it was all behind us
I am paying with my son again.
My son,
who sits and stares
and I don't know why.
Who sits and stares and sings Christmas carols,
obscene Christmas carols
and doesn't hear me when I talk.
And I don't know why, because he won't tell me what's
wrong,
and I can't ask him.
And I don't know why.
I don't know why.

And they ask me "why?" and I don't know why.
I don't know why.

    (*Blackout.*)

VIXEN

Yes, it's me.
Vixen.

You've heard so much talk about me,
you probably feel like you know me already.
Well, you don't.

You don't know what it's like
to be the world's most famous *victim*.
Y'don't know what it's like to have *your* name
used as a political rallying cry.
'Remember Vixen!'
I don't want to be remembered for this.

Y'don't know what it's like to have your sexual history
investigated.
... And probed
and examined and researched and the results tabulated
& scored, & published in all the newspapers.
In the Entertainment section.
Right under ' *What happened on your favorite soaps.*'

Y'don't know what it's like to have a USA Today phone-
in poll decide whether you are
just another helpless female,
or the Wench who stole Christmas.
Y'don't know what it's like
to have your *gynecologist*
interviewed on Geraldo.
'Does she have the kind of vagina that
this would happen to,
or does she have the kind of vagina that was just asking
for trouble?'

Y'don't know what it's like to be asked:
"Were you really raped,
or are you just trying to get back at Santa
because you are unhappy with your job?"
"Were you really raped
or are you trying to get attention for yourself?"

WAS I RAPED OR AM I UNHAPPY AT WORK???
WAS I RAPED OR AM I LOOKING FOR ATTENTION??????

I have never
had to work *this* hard
to get attention.

Call it a knack.
I remember one summer I was at a benefit at the Playboy
Mansion,
and Hef saw me and asked if I would do a photospread
for the December issue.
That got everybody's attention,
and I didn't even have to take off my clothes.
I wore the same kind of outfit we wear every Christmas
Eve,
only black leather.
And spikes instead of sleigh bells.
Boy, did that cause an outrage.
You'd think I'd *slept* with that hockey team.
Mrs. Claus threw a fit.
She wanted to have me fired.
No, actually she wanted to have me stuffed and
mounted,
but she was willing to settle for having me fired.
And branded with a scarlet "A".
I think she was just jealous
because she doesn't look good in a black leather harness
and spikes.

She doesn't look good in gold body paint and pasties,
either.

But that's what she wore to the office Christmas party
last year. Gold paint,
pasties
and an elf
strapped to her crotch like a fig leaf.
A screaming, terrified fig leaf.
I think she had planned to come as a Christmas ornament,
but, y'know, after that first pint of bourbon,
her creative juices get a little sloppy.
She staggered into that room.
And her elf screaming:

   (Fig leaf gesture.)

"AAH AAH AAH"
'Guess what I am!"

"You're a holiday fruitcake, honey."
That's what Cupid said.
And she spent the rest of the party hanging on all the
bucks, saying, "If I was a fruitcake, would you eat me for
Christmas?"
This is the woman who wanted me fired for moral
turpitude.
Apparently,
promiscuity is acceptable
as long as it's vulgar, humiliating
and ultimately futile.
That's a healthy attitude:
"Remember, girls:
A woman is only a slut
if she meets with some degree of success."

Despite Mrs. Claus's demands for my excommunication,
Santa did *not* fire me after I appeared in Playboy.

Instead, he offered me cunnilingus —
He's always been such a tasteful man.
I told him I thought his wife

was the one who really needed a tongue lashing.
Or a pistol-whipping.
Or to be left for dead the next time we find her out on
the icecap face down in the tundra after an eggnog binge.

It's hard for me to like a woman who enjoys taxidermy.

But then, this isn't about her.
It's about me, isn't it?
Am I telling the truth?
Or am I a lying vixen?
Did I seduce Santa with my reindeer wiles
so that I could blackmail him for better work conditions?

Did I lure him into the toyshop and force him to make
violent, sadistic love to me?
And what did I do to Rudolph?
What kind of animal am I??
Well, let's find out.
Let's just get to the bottom of this, right now.

"Vixen, do you promise to tell the truth the whole truth
and nothing but the truth so help you God?"
Absolutely, but I don't believe in God.
"Santa Claus believes in God."
God's been very good to Santa Claus.
"If it comes down to his word against yours,
you understand why we would have to believe *him?*"
Absolutely,
because Santa might be struck by lightning
if he were to tell a lie.
It's too bad God doesn't have the same policy for sex
offenders.

"Vixen, have you ever been arrested for possession of a
controlled substance?"
Yes.
Have you ever had sexual relations with anyone other
than your husband?"

After he died, absolutely.
"Since the death of your husband,
how many times have you had sexual intercourse?"
... More than once.
"How many different sexual partners have you had?"
Are you going to ask me if I was attacked?
"We want to establish your character, first."
What about Santa Claus's character?
"His character is beyond question."
Until a few days ago, so was mine.

"How many sexual partners have you had?"
... More than one.
"Have you ever had sexual relations with a woman?"
... Yes.
"Have you ever had sexual relations
with more than one partner at the same time?"
... Yes.
"Did you sleep with that hockey team??"

... Not all of them.

"How many members of the hockey team *did* you sleep
with?"
Why are you asking me these stupid questions??
You wanna crucify me, let's get to the good stuff!
Did I know that Santa had sexual fantasies about me?
Absolutely.
Did I let that prevent me from dressing in a provocative
manner when I was in his presence?
Not at all.
Did I know that he kept one of my pinups in his office in
the toyshop?
Yes.
Did I know that he used it to arouse himself during
masturbation? Yes.
Did I know that reindeer who have entered the toyshop
when he was in such a state of arousal had been groped
and molested?

64

Did I know that still other reindeer are rumored to have
been raped or sodomized in that same toyshop?
Yes!

Did I know that Santa Claus was in a state of arousal
when I walked into the toyshop that day?
Did I know what he had in mind when he came out of
his office?
When he took his whip down off the wall?
When he stood between me and the doorway?
Did I know that if I didn't kick him in the face and run
screaming from the toyshop before he even laid a hand
on me,
that I never would?
Yes!
I did!
How stupid of me!
I deserved to be raped.
I deserved it.
Why doesn't someone just fuck me right now?
I should have known better.
I should just stay away from the toyshop when Santa is
aroused. And since I'm not a mind reader,
I should just stay away from the toyshop.
Maybe I should stay away from the North Pole,
anyone stupid enough to go near it deserves to be fucked.

I should just not be on this planet
anytime it's possible that Santa Claus might be aroused,
that's the only smart thing to do.
Anyone who doesn't is asking to be fucked!

So I'm moving to Florida.
I've always hated the cold here.
I'm not pressing charges.
No one is going to believe me.
My only witness is a little red-nosed reindeer
who is in catatonic shock
because he walked in at the wrong time and saw

something he never thought he'd see again.
Who's gonna believe that?

Who wants to believe it?

And if anyone did believe me, then what?
I don't need
the end of Christmas-as-we-know-it
on my conscience.
That would be the perfect end to a very terrible week.

And I know some of the advocacy groups who have been
calling me, are going to feel like I've betrayed them.
I'm sorry.
But I've already done my part.
I was raped.
I gave at the office.
Let someone else do the paperwork.

I've asked Blitzen not to go through with the walk-out.
The toys will go out on Christmas Eve as scheduled.
My Christmas present to you:
A normal Christmas.

At the press conference tomorrow I will announce my
resignation.
I will not answer any questions,
and Santa Claus
will undoubtedly be cleared of the charges against him.

Then I'm going to Florida.
Where *I* can be normal again.

... Do I think my decision to leave
is going to make the world a better place?
A place where women and children can feel safe at
night?
A place where this sort of thing doesn't happen anymore?

Absolutely not.
Goodbye.

> (*Blackout. Three full seconds of silence. End of play.*)

• • •

NEW PLAYS 1995

ALICE IN LOVE
AN EVENING OF CULTURE: (FAITH
COUNTY II)
ASHES TO ASHES, CRUST TO CRUST
CINDERELLA: IT'S OKAY TO BE
DIFFERENT
FACE 2 FACE
HIDE AND SHRIEK
MY MOM'S DAD
ONCE UPON A BEGINNING
QUEEN FOR A DAY
REMOVING THE GLOVE
REUNION
STIFF CUFFS
THE EXPLORATORS CLUB
THIRTEEN PAST MIDNIGHT
VOICES 2,000
WINNING MONOLOGUES FROM THE
BEGINNINGS WORKSHOP

NEW PLAYS 1996

BEAUTIFUL GIRLS AND OTHER
WINNING PLAYS
BUTLER DID IT, AGAIN!
DICKENS' CHRISTMAS CAROL
GIRLS TO THE RESCUE
GRAND CHRISTMAS HISTORY OF THE
ANDY LANDY CLAN
LITTLE MATCH GIRL
PRINCESS PLAYS
SANDBAG STAGE LEFT
SGANARELLE
SNAPSHOTS
SNOWBALL AND OTHER PLAYS
TRIPLE DATE
TURN AROUND

Breinigsville, PA USA
18 February 2011
255830BV00004B/7/P